P9-DTE-721

Rosie's FIDDLE

By Phyllis Root

Illustrated by Kevin O'Malley

LOTHROP, LEE & SHEPARD BOOKS
New York

First Edition   1 2 3 4 5 6 7 8 9 10
Library of Congress Cataloging in Publication Data
Root, Phyllis.
Rosie's fiddle / by Phyllis Root; pictures by Kevin O'Malley,
p. cm.
Summary: Rosie O'Grady can out-fiddle the devil himself, say her
neighbors, and one day the devil challenges her to a contest.
ISBN 0-688-12852-1. — ISBN 0-688-12853-X (lib. bdg.)
[1. Violins—Fiction. 2. Devil—Fiction.]
I. O'Malley, Kevin, 1961-, ill. II. Title. PZ7.R6784Ro
1997 [E]—dc20 93-37430
CIP AC

For Mary and crazy women everywhere
—PR

For Giovanna,
who has battled the devil more than anyone I know
—KO

I f Rosie O'Grady ever smiled, no one but her

chickens had ever seen it. She was as lean and

hard as a November wind, as prickly as the roses

that grew by her door. She lived by herself on the

edge of town and liked it that way. The townsfolk

nodded and left her be. The only ones that came

near Rosie's place were the crows that pestered

her corn. . . .

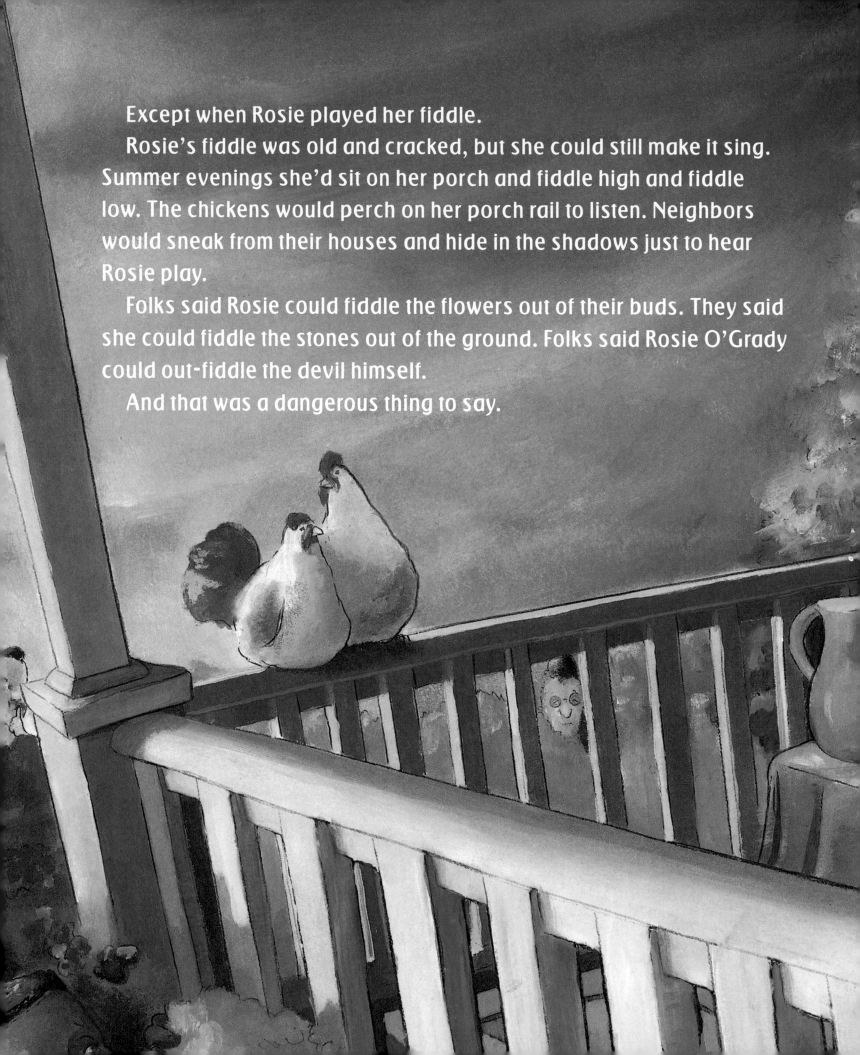

Except when Rosie played her fiddle.

Rosie's fiddle was old and cracked, but she could still make it sing. Summer evenings she'd sit on her porch and fiddle high and fiddle low. The chickens would perch on her porch rail to listen. Neighbors would sneak from their houses and hide in the shadows just to hear Rosie play.

Folks said Rosie could fiddle the flowers out of their buds. They said she could fiddle the stones out of the ground. Folks said Rosie O'Grady could out-fiddle the devil himself.

And that was a dangerous thing to say.

One day, Rosie was feeding her chickens when up walked a fine young fellow with a shiny bright fiddle in his hand.

"Good day to you, Ma'am," the young man said. "I hear you're a mighty fine fiddler."

Now Rosie knew right away who she was talking to. His hat was on crooked on account of his horns, and the tip of his tail hung out from under his coat. But she never let on that she knew.

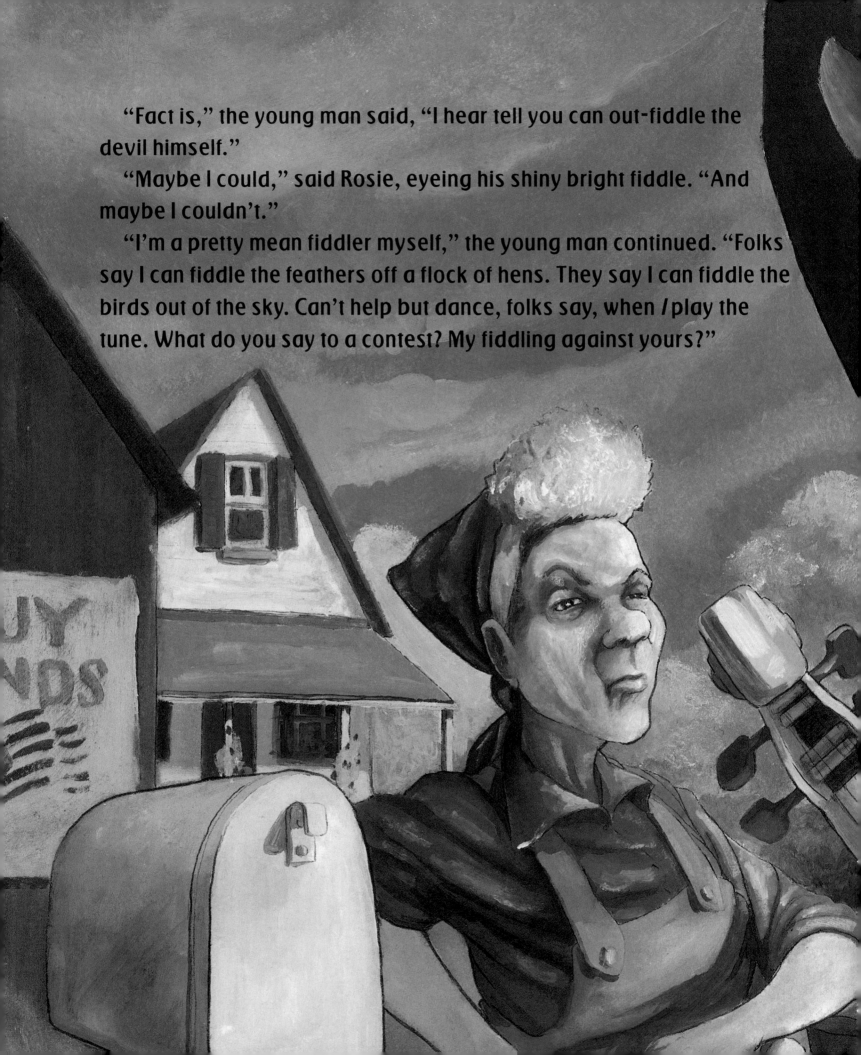

"Fact is," the young man said, "I hear tell you can out-fiddle the devil himself."

"Maybe I could," said Rosie, eyeing his shiny bright fiddle. "And maybe I couldn't."

"I'm a pretty mean fiddler myself," the young man continued. "Folks say I can fiddle the feathers off a flock of hens. They say I can fiddle the birds out of the sky. Can't help but dance, folks say, when I play the tune. What do you say to a contest? My fiddling against yours?"

"What would we fiddle for?" Rosie asked.

"You out-fiddle me, you can have one thing of mine," the young man said. "I out-fiddle you, I can have one thing of yours."

Now Rosie wasn't any fool. She knew what the devil would ask for if she lost: It was her soul she'd be fiddling for. But Rosie had a hankering for the devil's shiny bright fiddle.

"Done," she said and went to get her fiddle.

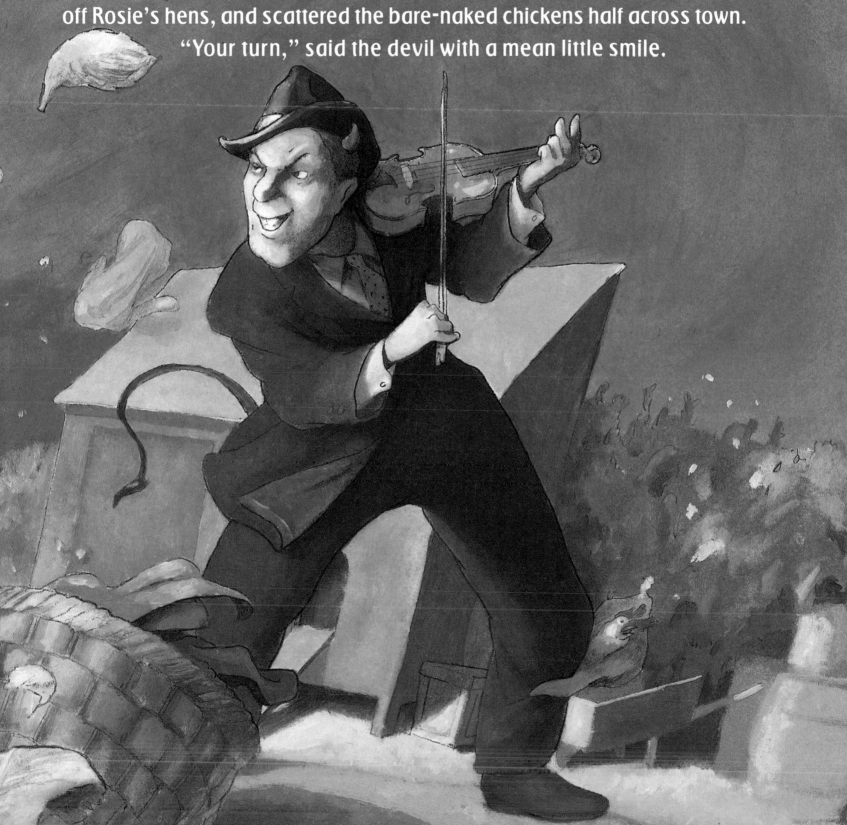

"Three times," said the devil, "and the best two's the winner." He picked up his bow and commenced to play.

Up came a wind, whining like the fiddle strings. It whipped the laundry from the line, snatched up the flowers like last year's leaves, blew the feathers off Rosie's hens, and scattered the bare-naked chickens half across town.

"Your turn," said the devil with a mean little smile.

Rosie tucked her fiddle under her chin, tuned a string, and started to play, sweet and high.

Along came a soft little breeze. It tickled the roses out of their buds, shook out the laundry and folded it up, then gathered the chickens and shooed them home.

"That's one for you," scowled the devil. "But I'm not out-fiddled yet."
He tightened his bow and began to play.
Faster and faster he fiddled, till a big black crowd of crows came
scooting across the sky.

Hundreds of crows. Thousands of crows. All with their beady black eyes on Rosie's corn. Beaks clacking, feathers flapping, they settled down for a feast.

"Your turn," sneered the devil, and his mean little smile got bigger and meaner. "Out-fiddle that!"

Rosie lifted her bow. She fiddled fast, and she fiddled hard. Pretty soon the rocks in that cornfield started skipping and rolling and hopping around. They rattled and clattered and hammered and banged. But the feasting crows didn't ruffle a feather. When they finally flapped away, not a kernel of corn was left in Rosie's field.

"One for me!" hooted the devil. "I'm not out-fiddled yet!"

By this time the townsfolk had come creeping out on their porches and slipping down to their gates to see what was going on. The devil saw them, and he smiled a big, mean smile as he raised his fiddle. "Can't help but dance," he laughed, "when I play the tune."

The first few notes he played, folks' feet started tapping. The next few notes, and they were kicking and twirling. Even the chickens were squawking and spinning. Pretty soon the whole town was dancing to the devil's fiddling—whether they wanted to or not.

The devil, he fiddled till everyone dropped. Then he put down his bow with the biggest, meanest smile yet.

"Can't nobody out-fiddle that," jeered the devil, and he reached for Rosie O'Grady.

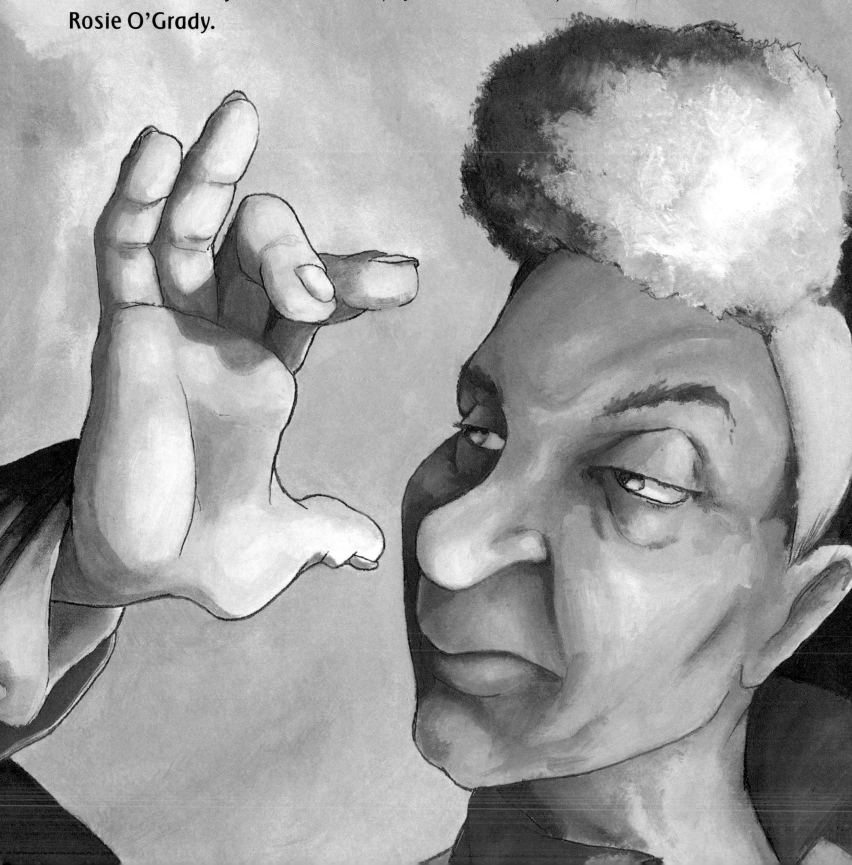

"Not so fast," said Rosie, and she started to fiddle.

She fiddled high, and she fiddled low, harder than she'd ever fiddled before in her life. Before long the devil's big toe started twitching. Pretty soon his heels started drumming. Next thing you know, he was leaping and prancing and hopping around—whether he wanted to or not.

"Stop!" shrieked the devil.

But Rosie fiddled on. Up flew his hat. Off flew his coat.

"You win," the devil gasped. "Just stop fiddling!"

But Rosie just fiddled faster and faster. The devil, he danced faster and faster, until *pfffft!* All that was left was a whiff of smoke and a shiny bright fiddle lying on the ground.

The townsfolk cheered. The chickens clucked.
And Rosie O'Grady smiled.

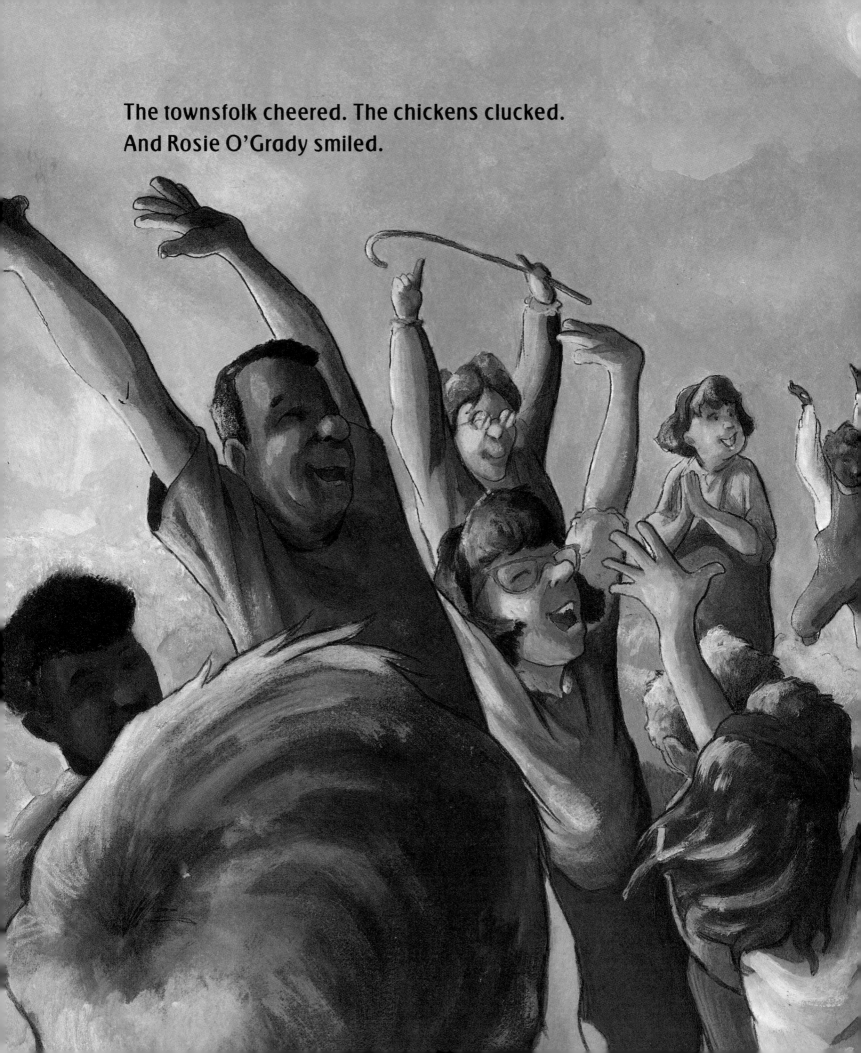

Folks still talk about the day Rosie O'Grady out-fiddled the devil himself. They tell about the scarecrow she made from the devil's hat and coat. Keeps away every crow in town, they say.

But mostly on a summer's night,
folks just gather at Rosie's place
and listen to her play her shiny new fiddle.